배수아

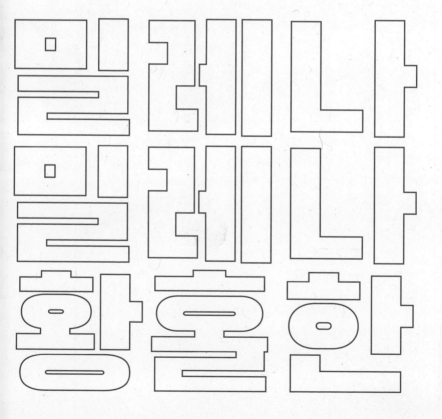

밀레나
밀레나
황홀한

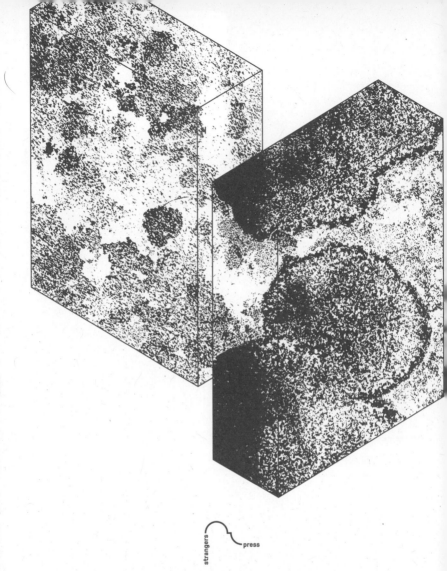

strangers press

UEA PUBLISHING PROJECT
NORWICH

BAE SUAH

MILENA, MILENA, ECSTATIC

Milena, Milena, Ecstatic
Bae Suah

Translated from the Korean by
Deborah Smith

First published by
Strangers Press, Norwich, 2019
part of UEA Publishing Project

Distributed by
NBN International
10 Thornbury Road
Plymouth PL6 7PP
t. +44 (0)1752 202301
e.cservs@nbninternational.com

Printed by
Swallowtail, Norwich

Series editors
Nathan Hamilton & Deborah Smith

Editorial assistance
Senica Maltese

Cover design and typesetting
Glen Robinson

Illustration and Design Copyright © Glen Robinson, 2019

ISBN: 978-1-911343-63-9

Yeoyu ——
new voices
Korea

TRANSLATED BY DEBORAH SMITH

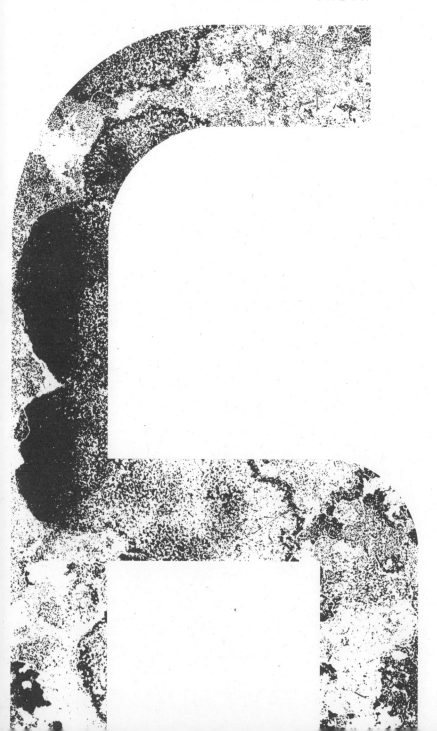

MILENA, MILENA, ECSTATIC

Hom Yun gets up and makes the first coffee of the day.

His method for making coffee is very simple: disliking all forms of coffee machinery, he puts three spoonfuls of extremely fine grounds into a cup and carefully pours in water boiled on the gas hob. Then he waits for around five minutes, until the majority of the powder has settled at the bottom of the cup, and takes a couple of sips to test that the coffee is sufficiently strong but not too hot, having had a little time to cool. Inevitably, a few coffee granules make their way into his mouth and a hint of graininess remains on his tongue. Hom Yun wraps both hands around the cup and waits in vain for the granules to subside as they float around the surface; fine and sticky as black mud, there is no way for them to sink completely – it is fate that some will be too dense to dissolve.

After taking another sip, he adds more water – as though it has only just occurred to him to do so. Hom Yun likes to start the day slowly and does so by very slowly drinking coffee. He begins with strongly concentrated coffee, which gradually becomes more diluted, as the temperature too follows an uneven but gradual downward trend. Cold coffee doesn't bother him especially. The only thing that irritates him are adulterations of metal and rubber packaging, the dregs of rust, the tastes of having been passed through a machine. Coffee that has been passed through a machine, or heated electrically, has a distinctive taste, as does water heated by the coil of an electric kettle. On his occasional visit to a café, he only ever drinks espresso – it's the only kind of coffee whose flavour is strong enough to neutralise the taste of machine. He always orders two singles rather than one double, drinking one first, then the other, so as to experience the difference in temperature, foam and mouthfeel – just like he does at home. If it happens to be a mild day, when the cries of the collared dove can be heard, he sets the cup on the table by the window, so the coffee receives the morning light. Cold coffee doesn't bother him especially. Neither does the feel of the fine granules against his tongue and against his throat.

He pours more hot water into the cup, adding another spoonful of powder. Giving the cup a swirl, he waits for the powder to subside. He repeats this process several times. Eventually, the coffee settles and, as he takes a sip, Hom Yun can see through to the bottom of the cup – to where a thick deposit has formed. He sighs, regretfully; he examines the sediment through the glass bottom. This unsurpassably soft thing, like sand shaped by ages of waves into concentric patterns; its lukewarm, delicately metallic scent; grey that appears dark red where deep brown shadows fall; silver speckles glittering dark and dazzling, like a distant nebula; this thing that endows the day with such significance.

Hom Yun's breakfast is also simple. Rather than corn cereal, crunchy and light as wings but which milk turns into a mush almost straight away, he prefers Swiss-style muesli made from dried oats, with yoghurt. His process for making breakfast is much simpler than that for making coffee. He pours muesli with dried fruit into a large soup bowl. He tops it with low-fat yoghurt. He eats.

Having drunk the coffee and finished the bowl of muesli, Hom Yun puts on a hat, laces up his trainers and heads out to the nearby park. A path runs between the dense trees. The clear cry of a blackbird with a golden beak. Then Hom Yun runs. Not very quickly but at a fixed tempo, along the same route he takes

MILENA, MILENA, ECSTATIC

every morning. In the stillness of the wood, only his breathing is audible, until two women flit past him on their bicycles. Until a man wearing a blue poncho made of coarse cloth grazes past from the opposite direction. Until he encounters a couple walking a dog at the very edge of the wood. Until the whimper and hum of a nearby drainage pump.

But Hom Yun runs. In the wood, there are crows and frogs, beeches and fresh poppies. But this same wood also contains the barbed wire fence of a substation, bottles of beer that have been tossed into the bushes and dirty swamps quietly rotting, covered in brown reeds. When he passes the gentle hill, his breathing becomes more laboured. He slows to get his breath back as a horse approaches from the opposite direction. A silver horse, close to white, with an even more striking and unusually white mark on its forehead, neither tearing up the grass nor being driven in harness by a coachman. It approaches at a swift gallop, facing straight ahead, and does not pay Hom Yun the least attention. He stops in his tracks and watches it pass with wondering eyes. He moves aside as the horse brushes by him in an instant. It vanishes into the woods on the opposite side of the clearing before its thundering hoofbeats have had time to die away. As far as Hom Yun knows, no one raises horses in this wood and there are no stud farms in the area. This is the first time he's ever seen a horse at all on this path and one on its own is still more difficult to comprehend. The encounter leaves Hom Yun in a state of extreme excitation. His shirt and hair are soaked with sweat as he walks and before long a gang of cyclists come pedalling along the path, their fluorescent green shirts all of an identical style. They and their yellow helmets pass by in a line. The end of the path is visible up ahead. Hom Yun is pleasantly fatigued. The air, heavy like gelatine, sticks tenaciously to his

BAE SUAH

skin. A dog barks somewhere nearby. Clouds mass.

What Hom Yun loves most is reading a book while immersed in lukewarm water. He runs a bath not to wash himself so much as to have the pleasure of reading in it. There are also times, taking a bath in the evening, when he has a glass of wine. In his bathroom, there is a small bookcase. The lower shelf holds a towel, a bathrobe, a razor, old slippers and the like, while the very top shelf always holds a little over a dozen books, of slightly different kinds. Of course, he also reads in bed, on the sofa, at his desk, on the subway, in a café, and sometimes standing in the street, but the books he takes to the bath tend to start each day's reading.

There has to be a book within reach in any part of the house where Hom Yun spends a considerable amount of time. By his pillow or under it, on the sofa, on the desk where he writes and in a kitchen cupboard, in the bathroom bookcase and by the bathtub, there are always several books waiting for him. As a result, he usually has from three to, at most, a dozen books on the go at any one time, moving back and forth between them all. For example, reading Dante in the bathtub, a detective novel or history book in the bedroom; on the sofa, one or two pages at a time of an encyclopedia of ancient alchemy, which he opens at random, and on the subway a poetry collection by Whitman or Eliot.

When sitting in a café, he generally reads plays. Shakespeare, Pinter, Ionesco and Beckett. He enjoys whichever he happens to have in his hand, none more or less than any other. At such times, the people who stumble into his field of vision become, quite unbeknownst to themselves, actors giving an impromptu performance of the play he's reading. For example, the young woman diligently writing something on a postcard at the table next to him is in fact writing a message for him, Hom Yun: 'Hello, I just now woke from a long faint; I can't

MILENA, MILENA, ECSTATIC

remember anything. So if you happen to be someone who knows
me, could you tell me who I am?' There are also times, three or
four times a year and very late at night, on those rare days when
he telephones his mother in the countryside, when Hom Yun
opens a large, thick book printed in old-fashioned lettering. It is
the memoir of a seventeenth century nun, who fell into a kind of
trance state lasting several weeks, in which she neither ate nor
slept and witnessed continual visions.

Of course, there are a great many books in Hom Yun's house,
which are not kept always close to hand. The majority are ones he
has already finished, but there are also those which were put back
on the shelves after only a few pages and subsequently forgotten,
those which he stopped reading halfway through, those which
he read so long ago that turning to them again feels almost as if
for the first time, and those which do genuinely provide a fresh
experience as he had never yet so much as glanced at the first
page. The majority are books that he bought himself, but there
are also many he received as presents. Now and then, when he
feels like a change of mood, he takes a dozen new books from the
shelves at random and uses these to replace whichever ones are
currently on the bathroom shelves, by the sofa, in the kitchen,
on the desk, or by the bed. And then his world is renovated at
random. His life begins afresh from an arbitrary page. Since this
is a way for him to periodically introduce an element of chance
into his reading life, there are no books in his house which he has
categorically decided will give him no enjoyment whatsoever,
but if possible, he would like his shelves to hold only those books
which will provide a satisfying experience whenever he might
happen to slide them out with a cursory glance at the title.

Yesterday, Hom Yun replaced all the books on his bathroom
shelves in this manner. Every so often, the feeling strikes him

that the time has come for such an action. Now, with his body immersed in the water, he picks up the topmost book from the small pile balanced on the edge of the tub. The book is *Letters to Milena*. If Hom Yun's memory is correct, he neither bought it himself nor received it as a gift. In fact, he'd utterly forgotten that such a book was even in his house. Of course, he cannot claim to possess an extremely precise memory. He might have acquired it decades ago, when he'd been in the habit of buying several books at once from second-hand shops. Now and then, it is true, such books ended up stuffed into a bookcase and forgotten. But *Letters to Milena*, which Hom Yun has in his hand now, isn't old enough to belong to that phase. Judging by the font, the paper, and the condition of the cover, he can't have had it for more than three or four years. For a long time now, Hom Yun has written the date in the inside cover of any book he buys or receives as a gift and he is careful to make a note of the place or circumstances whenever these hold some special significance. For example: 'Bought in Seoul's S bookshop, 1995' or 'From M at a birthday party, 1979'. This serves usefully the dual purpose of recording the history of the books in his possession while also stating his ownership of them. And he has never forgotten to make such a record, not even when buying dozens of second-hand books in one go.

Hom Yun examines the inside cover. There, someone has written a sentence in German, in pencil. Stiff and crooked, as though the writer were not familiar with the German alphabet and had simply copied out the words, the handwriting scattered clumsily and slanted irregularly and in individual strokes that did not join up with each other.

'Ecstatic Milena'

There are no markings other than that single sentence, which

MILENA, MILENA, ECSTATIC

he absolutely had not written himself. This means that this book is not Hom Yun's.

In the front portion of the book are occasional passages faintly underlined in pencil, but the majority of the pages are free from such markings and give off the characteristic scent of new paper. The book's owner clearly had not read it through. Perhaps a visitor to Hom Yun's home had pulled the book from their bag by chance, spent a few minutes reading it, and then forgotten to put it back in their bag before leaving. Hom Yun knows what it's like to lose a book. Once, while travelling in the Gobi desert, he put his copy of V.S. Naipaul's *Magic Seeds* on the shelf of the minibus and forgot to take it with him when he alighted at his destination. It was one of only two books he had brought with him, and he'd been just about to start on it, so he regretted this loss very deeply. Asking around, he eventually managed to track down the bus driver, but the driver couldn't understand what it was he was asking and, in any case, by that time *Magic Seeds* had already disappeared from where Hom Yun had left it.

Hom Yun recalls the desolation and regret of that time. The owner of *Letters to Milena* might turn up at Hom Yun's house unannounced one day. Someone who had visited Hom Yun's house must be someone that Hom Yun knows. They would ask him if it's possible that they once left a book there. He ought to put the book back in the bookcase where he would be able to locate it easily if or when the owner returned. But right this moment, sitting peacefully in water, water just warm enough to be pleasant but which would soon cool to lukewarm, it doesn't seem such a bad idea to skim-read some letters that were sent to a woman called Milena. So Hom Yun opens the book whenever takes his fancy, as he always does, and reads part of a letter to a woman called Milena.

BAE SUAH

Wednesday 17th July, 1920, Praha.

*In your letter you wrote: Ano mas pravdu, mam ho rada. Ale F.,
i tebe mam rada ('That's right, what you say is correct. I like
him. But F., I like you just the same'). I read this sentence very
carefully. Studying each word closely, one by one. Lingering
especially over the word 'I'. If this is not true, you are not Milena.
If you are not Milena, then what on earth can I be? You wrote
this sentence in Wien and sent it to me in a letter; that is better
than coming to Prague and saying it to my face. That's right,
I am aware. I understand everything quite clearly. Perhaps I
understand far better than you do yourself. Even so, for some
reason I am far too weak to read this passage all the way through
to the end. And so I write this here, in this letter, for you to see.
Now we read this passage together, face to face. (Your hair is
brushing my cheek.)*

Only after the water has cooled completely does Hom Yun get
out of the bath. He stands in front of the mirror to shave. His
image in the mirror is unfamiliar as always and is growing more
so by the day. Not only his face. To be frank, though he has
certainly not gained weight, still the skin on Hom Yun's chest has
lost its elasticity and now sags, his limbs growing skinnier by
the day. When the wind blows his thinning hair is unmistakable.
Hom Yun is well aware that he is ageing, and that he has been
ageing, especially for the past few years, at a rate that cannot
be concealed.

   Gazing at his blank face in the mirror, Hom Yun shaves. One
morning, he may get up and find that he no longer recognises
his face. On such a day, like a salesman discovering that he
has metamorphosed into an insect, he will stare at the man in
the mirror as blankly as he is now. The reflection there will be

MILENA, MILENA, ECSTATIC

half-bald, half an old man. And at that precise moment, half
a step away from this stranger, as though he's just bumped
into someone on the subway and drawn back, his face as
expressionless as ever, he will feel for the first time in his life the
tangible truth that all the world's transformation and unfamiliarity
are truly as shocking as literature insists and, expressionlessly,
he will finish shaving. Perhaps that day will come far sooner than
Hom Yun's vague presentiment would have it.

Hom Yun gets ready to go out. He only ever wears black clothes;
an inflexible habit he has maintained for thirty years already.
Black t-shirt, black trousers, black belt and a black jacket. On
his back, a black pack and on his feet, black shoes. Depending
on the weather, a black felt hat or baseball cap. Each time he
visits a city in a foreign country, he makes sure to go to its
central museum. In the museum shop, he stocks up on identical
black t-shirts, fifteen at a time. He knows no better place for
obtaining identical black t-shirts than the central museum shop
in a large city. All over the world, in every major city's museum,
there are always black t-shirts, as though they have been put
there expressly for Hom Yun. Simple black t-shirts bearing the
characteristic pictogram or archaeological pattern of their
respective city.
    Hom Yun takes the stairs rather than the elevator to get down
to the bottom of the building. On the lowest floor, he passes
through a long corridor lined on both sides with numbered doors,
heading for the passage that connects to the neighbouring
building. To get into that building, you must pass through two
doors, which are generally left open. Hom Yun does not usually
encounter anybody and no one encounters him. Passing through
both doors and stepping inside the neighbouring building, the

corridor divides into two in front of an elevator: one which passes straight in front of the elevator and continues on, and one which is perpendicular. Taking the first option and going up half a flight of stairs, one arrives at the building's rear yard, shabbily decorated with formal flowerbeds; there, a small door opens onto the street, near the stop for the bus to the subway station. The apartment complex consists of various buildings laid out like a propeller rotating on an axis. There had been fewer buildings originally, but over time each space was filled with yet another apartment block and these individual blocks were joined up to their neighbours on both sides, making one enormous complex all connected at the ground floor. Since this meant a complicated labyrinth of identical-looking corridors, a mistake could easily see one lose their way. Just before exiting the complex proper, Hom Yun glances back over his shoulder. The moment his gaze meets the dark corridor's windows, beneath the dim electric lights, all secret eyelids lower, without exception.

Having arrived at the cultural foundation's offices, Hom Yun has his appointment checked at the entrance and presents his ID before entering and being greeted by the foundation's programme manager, who he has already met a few times. They sit facing each other at an enormous round table in a large and impressively appointed meeting room, and the programme manager offers Hom Yun his congratulations because his independent film proposal was selected for the cultural support programme, a fairly large amount of money provided by the foundation's parent company. Hom Yun's proposal was for a film set around the graves of the Scythians of the mountainous High Altai region. He had gone through the full application process – editing his autobiographical film and various as yet unused

MILENA, MILENA, ECSTATIC

footage into a single collage-style demo, casting actors to do the narration, and spending almost eight months embroiled in an issue over music copyright – but hadn't genuinely expected that he would end up the lucky winner and granted such a substantial chunk of funding. Partly this was because he had made only a few films, considering his age, and had zero track record when it came to prizes. On top of that, what he had planned was a film of two halves, one half blending fiction and documentary, the other a tone poem constructed around a lyrical narrative; with such a genre, even if the film were completed in a way that was faithful to the synopsis and, with luck, screened in a cinema or on television, the cultural foundation and parent company couldn't expect anything much in the way of indirect publicity. And yet Hom Yun's proposal had been selected as the best, despite him lacking even a single friend or colleague who could have recommended him to the foundation. Now, according to his own meticulous calculations, Hom Yun had enough money to devote at least two years to production on location in the Altai of south-east Russia, Kazakhstan, and the archaeological digs of the Scythians and Huns in north-west Mongolia.

Hom Yun estimated that a single filming assistant would be sufficient. He always wanted to work with the fewest people possible. Generally this was to save money, but hadn't he avoided taking up a university position and chosen to become a freelancer precisely so that he would be able to work alone? Hadn't that, in fact, been his chief consideration?

Handing Hom Yun a bundle of documents, the programme manager helpfully points out the various places where he needs to sign. Naturally, he should take his time and read the contracts again, slowly. Even though the programme manager already sent him the full details in an email. The programme manager phones someone and asks them to bring Hom Yun a coffee. A short while later, a young secretary in glasses appears.

'How are you thinking of organising your team?' the programme manager says.

'It's enough to have one assistant who knows how to work a camera,' Hom Yun replies. 'If someone else suitable happens to turn up, one more person would be okay. But the only time I'll need the help of a real specialist will be after I come back from location, editing the sound and images together.' Hom Yun thanks the secretary and takes a sip of the coffee.

'Will a single assistant really be sufficient?'

'Once I'm out there, it will be difficult to find anyone with experience working on a film, except for as a guide or driver.'

'In that case, how long will you actually spend in Central Asia?' the manager asks and again demands something briefly of the secretary. Some business matter unrelated to Hom Yun.

'I'm planning at least two years.'

'That long?' The manager makes a show of surprise.

'This type of work can't be done in a rush,' Hom Yun answers.

'Particularly as we're planning on using footage of almost all the locations in each of their seasons, all the different time zones and climates. And we might end up needing to alter quite a few parts in the script once we're out there as it's possible that we'll encounter things we hadn't expected, that we decide to include in the film. This was also clarified in the proposal, but my scenario is not a fixed blueprint and neither is the narrative. Though it's based around a fictional story, the plan is for it to be narrated and expressed in the form of a documentary. And part of that means always being open to impromptu, unforeseen work. So, in any case, I think that the slower the time can go, the better – as far from rushing as possible.' His tone suggests he

MILENA, MILENA, ECSTATIC

already knows the identity of this 'we'.

'I see.' The manager nods emphatically. 'It wasn't only the assessors who admired your proposal. Everyone connected to the foundation found it quite compelling. A girl setting out on a long journey to find the mother who abandoned her as a child, eventually ending up at the ancient Scythian graves – beautiful and yet mysterious, you know. But what I'm personally curious about is, is the girl's mother really an ancient Scythian queen? Or is it the poor clerk who treated her so coldly, the woman who is listed as her mother on all official documents? That part seemed extremely surreal. There are many people who want to know the answer to the riddle and are wondering how it will be realised visually.'

'Right now, I can't say more than what's in the scenario. I've decided to show it to the audience with an open ending first, and see what they make of it. Then once I'm on location I'll make various experiments around how to represent that part visually. I'm expecting it will all fall into place one way or another.'

'Ah, I see. That will be your art.' The manager nods again. When he continues speaking, his tone is a little more business-like. 'The foundation will start preparing the applications for your various visas and permissions of entry and, since these things are always a little drawn-out, you might want to start preparing for the trip in the meantime. And obtain the necessary assistant! Or perhaps you already have a team you usually work with?' the manager asked, circling back to his earlier query.

'No,' Hom Yun replied. 'I've always worked alone. Though now and then, when it's been necessary, I've hired a temporary assistant. But never for such a long-term project as this.'

The manager signals with his hand to the secretary, who stands there blankly and looking somewhat inexperienced, that it is okay for her to leave.

'You've filmed in Central Asia before… ?'

The secretary quietly leaves the meeting room, and the thick, heavy door closes quietly behind her.

'Five years ago, yes. In the Gobi desert, so not Central Asia exactly. It was my first project as a freelancer. A visual work based on the fables of Mongolia and northern China.'

'And did you go with a team then?'

'Yes, I did. That time… actually I did almost all of the work myself but, since I also needed to appear as an actor, I hired an assistant with some basic knowledge of how to operate the camera.'

Hom Yun's coffee cup is empty, and his signature fills each blank space that requires it.

Hom Yun heads for the subway station with the intention of returning home, only to abruptly switch direction; he decides instead to walk the early afternoon streets for a while. Having thought of little else lately, part of him wants to go straight home and continue working on his film scenario but, as he's already in the city, he also wants to enjoy a sliver of free time, to sit in a café with two cups of espresso.

The film Hom Yun plans to make will be ten hours long. At least, that will be his private version, which he will present to the foundation. The abridged theatrical version will be two and a half hours at most. For the past few years, he has been writing a lengthy monologue filled with wilderness, memories and hallucinations. With the prize money he can have this recorded as a voiceover by a professional actor. Now, he will be able to realise in language and images the scenario he's had in his mind

MILENA, MILENA, ECSTATIC

for several years, that he sketched out in fragments whenever he had a bit of spare time. Hom Yun is struck by a happiness so shocking it's close to vertigo. Yes, it is shocking. Always, the things that have fascinated and captivated him have tended to be those that shocked him.

Of course, he has also experienced the opposite kind of shock.

Somewhat excited, Hom Yun enters a café and orders two strong espressos, only then noticing a pang of hunger. He chooses a piece of brioche to go with them.

Hom Yun is not a heavy eater. In fact, not infrequently breakfast is his only meal of the day. At university, he weighed more than 90 kilograms. Whenever he sat at a dining table, he gorged himself. At 2am every morning, he drank a bottle of wine and either napped until the afternoon or didn't sleep at all. But since leaving, his habit of eating dinner later than most other people disappeared and his weight decreased. He deliberately reduced the amount of food and alcohol he consumed and still he goes jogging three times a week.

Acting in his own films had made him feel that there was a problem with how his figure appeared on screen. Of course, it was difficult to call it proper acting, as he had simply sat there with the camera pointed at him, his silhouette seen from behind, sitting with both hands above his head, wearing baggy poncho-type clothing and sunning himself on the banks of a river while the sun rose. Nothing more. He had chosen to perform himself because he couldn't afford to employ a professional actor on an independent film without any external backing and because it was impossible to find an actor who understood the script as well as he did – who realised with his body what Hom Yun held in his mind.

BAE SUAH

Slowly tearing off pieces of brioche while he works his way through the two espressos, one very slightly cooler than the other, Hom Yun watches the people walk by outside the window. He sees young men with leather backpacks and the most fashionable suits, tight enough to reveal the lines of their physique. Women pass by adorned and upholstered with makeup, artificial nails and eyelashes, chest padding, cosmetic contact lenses. There are also a fair number talking on phones. Hom Yun briefly imagines that it's his number being dialled by one of the young women in front of him. 'Hello, just now I woke up from a long faint; I have no memories at all. So if you happen to be someone who knows me, could you tell me who I am?' The feeling it gives him is not bad at all, actually quite exciting, and he plans to keep it going while reading a few pages of a play, as he always does in cafés. But what Hom Yun pulls out of his jacket pocket is not the collection of Beckett plays he's expecting, but again *Letters to Milena*. He's almost entirely certain he put it back on the shelf before leaving the house and can't understand how it's ended up here. The most likely explanation is that he's hallucinating. Or he could have been holding the Beckett in one hand and *Letters to Milena* in the other, intending to take the former out with him and put the latter back on the shelf, only to get them mixed up. No problem, Hom Yun thinks. Just for today, *Letters to Milena* will do as well as a play, since a letter is equally relevant to the actor's monologue.

One young woman is deep in thought, her faintly absent-minded stride carrying her so close to the café that her body almost touches the glass. She is of the usual height and body type, wearing green trousers, a very pale yellow blouse, and glasses. Hair falling down to her shoulders, pale white skin, with no artificial extras – neither lashes, nails, chest padding, nor

MILENA, MILENA, ECSTATIC

cosmetic contact lenses. Even her makeup is very light. In a word, she is ordinary. Ordinary not in the sense of average, but in the sense of a nonspecific majority among which it would be meaningless to attempt to make a distinction. One cannot conclude that she is not beautiful: ordinary beauty, that degree of beauty possessed by most young women, is also possessed by her, but she is beautiful not because she is a young woman but because she is ordinary. Possibly because hers is an impersonal ordinariness that no one could hate, too strong to be lorded over by a queen yet not strong enough to be pursued outside of a crowd. If her ordinariness were to have a character, that character would be darkness. A shadowed darkness, like a camera lens covered with black cellophane. Her red lips are dark. Her black hair is dark. Her black pupils behind her clear glasses are dark, and her white skin is dark. After standing for a while gazing inside the café, she pushes open the door with an air of resolve, orders a cup of black coffee, and takes a seat at a table not far from Hom Yun.

Hom Yun bows his head and opens *Letters to Milena*.

Milena, Milena, Milena – today I absolutely cannot write any other word. That's right, today in the circumstances of urgency and tiredness, and insensible existence (but this will be the same tomorrow too) the only name that is rising up is... Milena! (If I whisper in your left ear like this, you who are deeply asleep in this impoverished bed, knowing nothing at all, slowly turn from right to left bringing your skin close to my lips).

Hom Yun gets the feeling that someone is watching him, lifts his head and looks around. The café is half full, half empty. Everyone has a cup of coffee in their hand but no one is only drinking coffee. They are also having a conversation, either in person or on the phone; reading a book, writing on a computer, translating, writing a letter; gazing outside the window, briefly lost in thought; crying, kissing someone, or laughing. In other words, nothing special is happening, only what is ordinary. Hom Yun is just about to turn back to his book when his gaze alights on the table next to him, where a man and woman had been sitting just moments ago. There, one of them has left a film programme. Hom Yun reaches out and picks up the timetable without leaving his seat. It is the programme of a small cinema housed in the basement directly below the café, which specialises in old black and white films. It occurs to him that having come into the city centre, he might as well go to the cinema. And according to the programme, the next screening is about to start. Maybe that's why the couple hurried away. Hom Yun downs in one what little espresso remains in the bottom of his cup and jumps up from his seat. He dusts off the brioche crumbs with a single sweep of his hand, finds the steps leading down to the basement and strides down. After buying a ticket for the film and a cola at the small ticket-booth-cum-snack-bar, he gropes his way into the cramped, black theatre.

Hom Yun finds an empty seat. The woman in glasses appears and sits down in the seat next to his. She is breathing hard enough for Hom Yun to hear, as though she had been running so as not to miss the film. In response, the hallucination overtakes him that a woman's moist, warm heart and lungs are vibrating minutely right beneath his own skin. The film starts, drowning out the sound of any breathing. The naked flesh of a man and woman glitters like sand. Dialogue begins as a voiceover. *You saw nothing in Hiroshima*. The first scene of *Hiroshima Mon Amour* unfolds.

I was always starving, illegitimacy and adultery, lies and death...

MILENA, MILENA, ECSTATIC

The actress delivers her monologue.

When the film has ended and the lights come back up, Hom Yun finally recognises the woman next to him as the secretary he encountered that afternoon at the cultural foundation. He had only really seen her in passing, but it is beyond doubt that she is the same woman. They stare at each other for a while, blinking.

'Didn't we meet today at the foundation,' Hom Yun asks.

She nods without words.

'Running into each other again here, it's a strange coincidence,' Hom Yun says.

'I haven't eaten anything all day,' she responds.

After this exchange of not-quite greetings, they decide to go and have dinner together.

Outside, where darkness has already spread through the streets, they pass two men carrying guitars crossing the road. Both men are playing their instruments as they walk. Hom Yun and the woman stop in their tracks and stare at each other again. 'It truly is a strange coincidence,' Hom Yun says.

'It feels like I saw the same thing happen in the film just now,' she responds. Though perhaps it wasn't in today's film but one I saw a long time ago – no, perhaps it wasn't in a film at all that I saw it,' she tails off. As she speaks, the certainty gradually fades from her expression and unease blooms like a flower in its place. An initial assuredness that had seemed to captivate transforms into the uneasy expression of an ordinary woman who is about to have dinner with a man she doesn't know.

They go into the first restaurant that catches their eye. The pot on the external fireplace has just started to puff steam, and the proprietress lifts the lid to fish out the cooked dumplings. It's a dumpling restaurant. They order a mix of vegetable and meat dumplings. The woman fills two glasses with water and lines up two sets of chopsticks in front of Hom Yun and herself and pours soy sauce into two tiny bowls, adding wasabi and a good shake of red chilli powder. She performs these actions without any words and Hom Yun makes no move to prevent her though he doesn't like spicy food. A plate of steaming dumplings is set on the table in front of them. Hom Yun transfers one onto his empty plate. She does the same. They dip their dumplings in the soy sauce.

She asks the first question. 'When are you thinking of setting off on your filming trip?'

'I'm intending to leave when the visa's ready,' Hom Yun answers simply, 'but I've got various preparations to make first'.

'If I were to leave home for such a long time, how would I feel... I can't imagine,' she mutters as if talking to herself.

He tells her that he's been on several filming trips, becoming so familiar with being on the road for months at a time that he now thinks nothing of it, but that he's never yet been away for as long as he will be this time.

'I can't imagine,' she repeats after a pause. 'I really... can't imagine.'

'Life consists of the unimaginable,' Hom Yun says and then hesitates for a moment. Such an excessively conclusive manner of speaking seems unsuitable for a conversation with a young woman, but her expression does not change.

They eat dumplings in silence for a while. When they have almost cleared the plate, a radiant look steals over her face and she suddenly blurts out 'Being with someone... it's so great!'

Hom Yun pauses in eating to glance up at her. The hallucination again overtakes him that a woman's moist, warm heart and lungs are vibrating minutely right beneath his own skin.

At some point, they become the only customers in the

MILENA, MILENA, ECSTATIC

restaurant. The others all left at once, as though keeping some kind of appointment. The pot from which the steam had been billowing sleeps and the fire in the brazier goes out. Even the lighting in the restaurant grows dim. All the lights except those above their table have gone off, the rest of the room subsiding into shadows. Even the woman who had made the dumplings has hidden away in the kitchen from which a faint light seeps out. They hadn't noticed the window blind being lowered. This restaurant must only open at idiosyncratic times, Hom Yun thinks, after which the blinds are lowered and the lights turned off. Their plate of dumplings is empty. Hom Yun puts a note on the table to cover the price of the meal.

They leave and walk slowly towards the subway station. From somewhere or other comes the sound of singing and a tune played on a guitar. Possibly it is the street musicians they passed a little earlier. Hom Yun looks around to see if he can spot them; he can't. The woman hesitates briefly before addressing him.

'People say... they say you're a prodigy, Director Hom. No, don't laugh. It's what everyone at the foundation says. Don't deny it. You say 'prodigy' is only used to refer to young people? That it's better suited to young people like me? No, you're wrong. I'm not young at all. What I mean... if you aren't young, Director Hom, then neither am I. I'm not an age that could be called young. The even more conclusive factor is that I am nothing. Not only because I'm not a film director. Whatever aspect you consider, I am a perfect nothing. I'm not only saying this because I was a temp at the foundation. Yes, was – the contract was for six months. Today was my last day. So now I'm even more nothing than I was. The people at the foundation... I've heard them call you a prodigy. Also a hermit. Only ever making films on your own, but you don't want to be called a hermit? You really don't think the word applies to you? But if you're always on your own, and you're not afraid of that, well then, isn't that being a hermit? Whereas I'm often afraid... of being alone... I don't know much about films. But I saw yours. I... it was so great! Not that it can matter all that much what a person like me thinks about something that's already been praised by so many amazing people. I just felt I had to tell you this, if I ever got the opportunity. Your film was like a long poem. You heard people call it boring? Absolutely not. If I read the script again right now, I don't think I could hold back the tears. It was like a shocking poem. I know there's nothing especially sad or grand in the plot itself. Nothing that could be called a major event! Even so, I watched your demo film several times. I especially liked the conclusion, where it hints that the girl kills herself. She leaves her impoverished real mother, who doesn't love her, and heads off to the world of the ancient Scythians in search of her original mother. To a steppe kingdom whose history is unknown, because it was never recorded. No one thinks they cannot criticise such a suicide! I don't know much about films. But before I worked at the foundation I spent two years as an assistant writer at a small TV production company. So I know a bit about working with cameras, even though it wasn't on films. I never took any official courses, just picked things up on various shoots. At least the basic operating method. And the various ways of composing a scene... I'm familiar with that kind of sensory aspect. So I wondered, if you aren't able to obtain a suitable assistant, might you take me on this trip with you?'

Hom Yun is lost for words. The guitars start up again, off in some alleyway. Faint light, uneasy light, and the sounds of the guitar. These, the constituent parts of the surrounding night, flow from some unknowable place, bearing a part of himself and the woman away with them: the white steam that had billowed from the pot of dumplings; the restaurant owner whose expression could not be seen; the other customers eating in silence, who all left the restaurant at the same time, not speaking to each other even once, they had finished their dumplings, leaving only the two of them behind; the blind that had at some point been lowered over the restaurant's glass door; the owner who had disappeared inside the kitchen, her careful hand that had set the chopsticks side by side on the table and tilted the soy sauce bottle to pour from it. The pot sleeps and the fire in the brazier goes out.

This woman is not at all beautiful, Hom Yun thinks, gazing at her face; why have I listened to her for so long? Why am I waiting to hear what she will say next? No, it might not be fair to say that she is not at all beautiful. She is a young woman, after all. So maybe she is beautiful. But were that to be the case, it would be because of an expression that is hidden from her. Precisely that expression which her face does not assume.

Gazing at Hom Yun, the woman speaks again.

'Please take me with you. I'm well aware that a filming assistant is not a stable job. That the position disappears once filming is over. I'm also well aware that no future prospective employer will think that being an assistant on an independent film counts as work experience, especially a film that isn't even publicised, so anyone who doesn't work in film would advise me against me it, saying that it's a waste of time. But what does that even mean, a waste of time? Such words are not applicable to me. For me, there is no such thing as time. Time in its simplest sense was never something granted me. My only time is night. Like now. Night that goes on for a long, long time. Never-ending night.

BAE SUAH

My only time is that which is invisible, opaque, faint. If I keep still, I gradually get dispersed into the night like smoke, thinning out until I disappear so completely no one would know I was ever there. With no one able to know anything about me, that's how I will disappear. However little you pay me, I won't mind. In fact, money won't be necessary in the steppe. You say that the work will be difficult? I would be ecstatic. You say that I will have to sleep in a sleeping bag and do without showers or a bathroom? If I could go there, I would be ecstatic. If I stay here, my night never ends. If you would take me with you, I would be ecstatic.'

From the dim bottom of a deep place in the black night, her white face looks up at him. She stares piercingly at Hom Yun, her face all the time sinking and shrinking until it dwindles to a single white point invisible in the darkness. Hom Yun thinks he hears a scream, or was it the guitars again? Closing her eyes – 'sorry, I have vertigo' – the woman now reaches out and steadies herself against the nearest wall. Hom Yun takes hold of her arm, steers her over to some nearby steps and sits her down. They sit side by side gazing at the night streets.

'You seem like you have some reckless desire to run away,' Hom Yun says. 'What do you want to escape from?'

She ignores his question. Her boldness shifts to the unease of an ordinary woman sitting with a strange man in the middle of the night. She bends over and picks up the book that has fallen to the floor and in doing so her arm accidentally grazes Hom Yun's leg. He makes an awkward movement to avoid it which results in his hand coming to rest on her knee.

The book she now holds is *Letters to Milena*, its having fallen from Hom Yun's pocket, and she turns the pages for a while with her white hand before passing the book back to Hom Yun, nodding. She says she doesn't know how to read a foreign

MILENA, MILENA, ECSTATIC

language. She doesn't know who Milena is.

'Before I worked at the broadcasting company, I was a waitress at various restaurants downtown while attending college. I worked shifts at two, sometimes three restaurants in the same day. Going from this one to that. Ah, now I think about it I might even have worked at the dumpling place we just had dinner at. But that's not a precise memory. There were many restaurants where I only worked for a few days, you see. Some I left without saying a word, and some I was fired from since I wasn't a very diligent waitress. Every now and then, I would give the wrong change, or break a plate, or drop some food. I wanted to cry, you know. Wherever I was, whatever was going on, I was never able to feel 'at home'. But where was my home? Where had I come from? Who was I? I couldn't remember the slightest thing. However hard I try, I can't imagine it... I don't know who Milena is. I'm not Milena. And if I am, I don't know it. No one does. But please take me with you. You say it will be a long trip? I would be ecstatic.'

'I can't promise,' Hom Yun tells her, but he can't get a clear idea of the words coming out of his mouth. He only mutters repeatedly, reflexively, avoiding the woman's gaze, with both fists clenched as though in self-defence. I can't promise anything. I can't promise anything.

Hom Yun is struck by an unidentified fear. He feels that the woman is about to say to him: 'Hello, just now I woke from a long faint; I have no memories at all. So if you happen to be someone who knows me, could you tell me who I am?' Or perhaps: 'Hello, I was born to parents who hated each other. Naturally they didn't want me... apparently my mother left in despair over the fact that she was pregnant with me. They said she had another man. That she was an unfaithful woman. I don't know who my mother is. I have no memory of her face. But that didn't make me uneasy, because I had my father. One day my father took me out with him, holding my hand as usual; the place he took me to was the house of a relative and there, my father let go of my hand. I don't know where he went after that. After several years, the relative sent me to another relative. And then to another relative again. To a relative's relative's relative's relative... moving at ever shorter intervals to the houses of ever more distant relatives. The first man I ever embraced was some male relative, at one of that string of relative's houses. I don't know which relative was which, or whose house was whose. I was scared that I might be pregnant! Scared to death! I was surrounded by relatives who were too many, too distant, who brought ambiguity to the very concept of being related to someone. The relatives formed a whirling vortex around me. Holding each others' hands and spinning, as though they were all going to melt together like a single lump of butter. It gave me vertigo. Then one day, I suddenly ended up alone. I don't know where they all went. I don't know where I came from. I was standing at a bus stop with an old suitcase, wearing a coat that came all the way down to my ankles. The very same checked suitcase that always came with me when I moved from one relative's house to another. Was it a bequest from my father? Or from my mother? I don't know anything. Every now and then, I want to kill myself. If I did, I would be ecstatic. But ah, to be with someone... it's so great!'

'Stop that!' Hom Yun burst out. 'Stop going on and on about the same thing! It's annoying!'

Hom Yun glares straight at the woman. That is, he tries to glare straight at her. He tries to move the arm that has been touching her without him realising. He tries to pull away from her body. He tries telling himself how unpleasant he finds her hair incessantly brushing his face. He thinks of spelling it out to her:

MILENA, MILENA, ECSTATIC

I have to go now, whether you're alone or not. I don't care a thing
about you. But all of a sudden she is not there. She has already
wandered away, following the faint guitar melody trickling out
from some alleyway. There are people, seen from behind, moving
further away into the darkness in front of him. There is a wavering
shadow. There is the sound of footsteps on the pavement. It is
a cloudy night. There are the people moving away, seen from
behind. What was I? Where did I come from? Please take me there
with you. I would be ecstatic. It is a cloudy night. There are the
long shadows of people moving away. One of them is probably her.
She whose name he does not know. Milena.

Hom Yun stands at the entrance to his apartment complex. When
he steps inside, the doors lining both sides of the dark corridor
are gloomy in the faint light. The scene is the same as when he
left home this morning. The unchanging apartments that have
always been the same, both yesterday and the day before. Late
at night, his footsteps sound unusually loud in the corridor. The
shadow of a plant wavers in the window of one apartment, its
huge leaves like outstretched fingers. A cat cries. Water running
from a tap cries. Crickets and window frames cry, delicately. A
long-legged night spider cries. A grey moth with transparent
wings cries, its whole life spent trapped in insect window mesh.
Drifting dreams cry. The cries of all of these things spread to fill
the corridor. Wobbling a little, Hom Yun hurries down its length. He
doesn't encounter anyone, and no one encounters him.

    He passes mutely in front of door after door without turning
to look at any of them. But when he arrives in front of the elevator
he finds himself gazing into a mirror. The mirror is darkly tinted,
stained at the edges, and cracked into three pieces. He stares
without expression at his own cracked, unfamiliar face. He doesn't

encounter anyone, and no one encounters him. He asks no one about themselves, and no one will ask him about himself.

Hom Yun closes his eyes so as not to see his own cracked face. In the mirror, a person passes behind him wearing a red coat, gazing briefly at Hom Yun's face in the mirror, his closed eyes.

In life, there are these single moments.

The cracked face of the person stares at the cracked unseeing face of Hom Yun and the person turns and walks away, their reflection in the mirror moving further away as they walk up to the very end of the corridor, open the last door and step inside, disappearing inside their home. Before crossing over to the next building, where he lives, Hom Yun turns and looks behind him. As always, when he turns his gaze on them, the doors all have their eyelids lowered.

Back at his own apartment, Hom Yun discovers a scrap of paper that has been pushed under his door. He picks the paper up and reads it, standing in the entrance-way. He reads it three times. He turns to go back out, then stops. For a while, he cannot move, as though unable to decide what he ought to do. In the end, he goes inside, takes off his jacket and hangs it over the back of a chair. He goes into the kitchen and checks whether there's any coffee left over from breakfast, but the cup holds only a thick heap of dried dregs. Sighing, he looks inside the fridge, where he discovers some cola, which he drinks straight from the bottle. Hom Yun sits on the sofa. He tucks his legs up onto it and lies down. The wall clock ticks. If he listens carefully, he can hear that the second hand moves at an irregular speed. It's as though he can hear many clocks all going at different speeds, an incredible palimpsest of sound. Time gets recklessly amplified, gradually filling the interior of the apartment, transparent but with volume, like water. Hom Yun puts his hands over his ears

MILENA, MILENA, ECSTATIC

and closes his eyes as though to block out the sound of time. The clock ticks. The tap in the bathroom drips. The fridge hums and vibrates. The water in the kettle sways and sloshes. The desk and table and doorframe creak and cry dryly. Somewhere, a cat begins to cry again. The spider cries. The moth cries. In this overcast night... he jumps to his feet and puts on his jacket. He goes out again. Hom Yun takes the stairs rather than the elevator to the bottom of the building. On the lowest floor, he passes through a long corridor lined on both sides with numbered doors, heading for the passage that connects to the neighbouring building. To get into that building you must pass through two doors. These are usually left open. Hom Yun generally does not encounter anybody, and generally no one encounters him. Only after he crosses into the adjacent building and arrives in front of the cracked mirror next to the elevator does he stop for a moment to get his breath. His profile appears in the mirror, then slides away as he changes direction.

In the mirror, he turns around and walks away. His reflection recedes in the cracked mirror. His existence is gradually wiped out. He walks to the end of the corridor and stands in front of the very last door. He hesitates, then rings the bell. In the mirror, he is very small. The door opens, and the cracked, vague night mirror watches, from a distance, as someone invites him into the apartment.

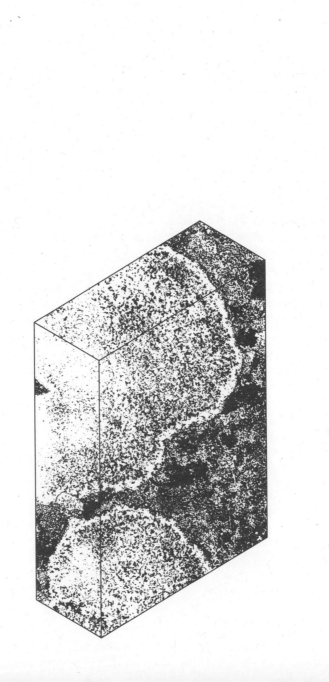

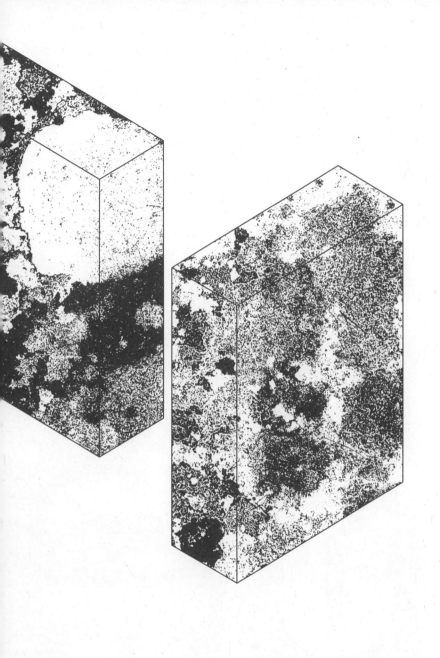

Yeoyu is a series of chapbooks showcasing the work of some of the most exciting writers working in Korean today, published by Strangers Press, part of the UEA Publishing Project.

여유

Yeoyu is a unique collaboration between an international group of independent creative practitioners, with University of East Anglia, Norwich University of the Arts, and the National Centre for Writing, made possible by LTI Korea.